Annie Oakley

One of the greatest sharpshooters that ever lived was a woman. When Annie Oakley was a little girl, her father taught her to use a gun. When she was 9 years old, she went off to hunt on her own and came back with a squirrel. She also came back with a black eye, because her rifle kicked back and hit her.

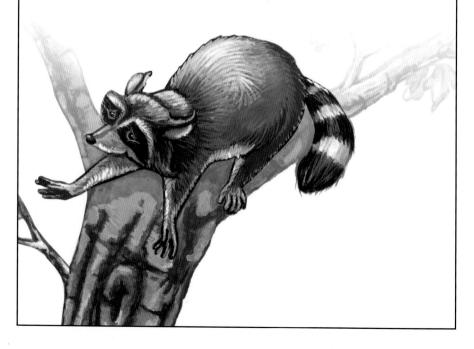

As a teenager, Annie became a great hunter and even sold her takes at the market. She became so well known, that she took part in shooting matches. One day, she competed against a professional marksman named Frank Butler. Even though she was 10 years younger than him, she won!

Frank was very impressed with the young girl's skill, so he invited Annie to take part in one of his marksman shows.

As part of the act, Frank shot an apple off of his dog's head.

The dog, named George, was a big hit with audiences—and with Annie.

Frank traveled all over the country with his act, but he kept in touch with Annie, writing letters from many different places. They soon fell in love and were married.

Annie continued to practice shooting.

Frank decided to ask his wife to take part in his show. The crowds were always impressed by the small, pretty young woman who could shoot out the center of a playing card without any effort at all. The applause was deafening when she ended the show by shooting a cigarette from Frank's mouth.

The couple toured the country, along with George, showing off their marksmanship. Everywhere they went, the audience would hold its breath as they watched the dangerous stunts.

As soon as the bullet hit its mark, the crowd erupted in applause and cheers.

One day, the famous Sioux Indian chief, Sitting Bull, was among the spectators. He became a great fan of Annie's shooting skills and they became friends.

His nickname for her was "Little Sure Shot" and he said that her eyes were as sharp as an eagle's.

A few years later, Annie and Frank joined the famous Buffalo Bill's Wild West show.

This show was an exciting mix of plays with cowboys and Indians, wild animal stampedes, and Native American dances. Annie was usually the first act, right after the opening parade.

During their time with Buffalo Bill and his show, Annie and Frank traveled around for 17 years.

They even crossed the ocean to go to England for the 50th anniversary of Queen Victoria's reign. In fact, Annie was invited to Buckingham Palace to meet the Queen in person!

When the Wild West
show toured Europe,
it stopped in Germany
where it performed for
the Emperor and his son,
Crown Prince Wilhelm.
The Crown Prince asked
Annie to shoot a cigarette
from his mouth.

Imagine how nervous
Annie was as she took
careful aim and fired. As
usual, she made the shot.

Annie continued shooting after
leaving the Wild West show.
When she won contests, Annie gave
the money to charities that helped
poor children. On her sixty-second
birthday, Annie shot a hundred clay
targets in a row, just to show that
she was as good a shot as ever.

Annie Oakley died in 1926, at the age of 66. She will always be remembered as a woman who chose a life of excitement and adventure at a time when most women were expected to stay home and raise families.